Running Press Kids
Hachette Book Group
1290 Avenue of the Americas, New York, NY 10104
www.runningpress.com/rpkids
@RP_Kids

Printed in China

First Edition: November 2020

Published by Running Press Kids, an imprint of Perseus Books, LLC,
a subsidiary of Hachette Book Group, Inc. The Running Press Kids name
and logo is a trademark of the Hachette Book Group.

The Hachette Speakers Bureau provides a wide range of authors for speaking events.
To find out more, go to www.hachettespeakersbureau.com or call (866) 376-6591.

The publisher is not responsible for websites (or their content)
that are not owned by the publisher.

Print book cover and interior design by Marissa Raybuck.

Library of Congress Control Number: 2019953746

ISBNs: 978-0-7624-6973-4 (hardcover), 978-0-7624-6972-7 (ebook),
978-0-7624-7014-3 (ebook), 978-0-7624-7015-0 (ebook)

APS

10 9 8 7 6 5 4 3 2 1

For my parents.
— **K. L.**

For my mom, the greatest superhero I know.
— **R. V.**

Everybody knows that being a superhero
is hard and messy work.

Superheroes:
Fight evil!

Catch bad guys!

Help people (and animals)!

Save the day!

Everybody knows that superheroes wear: Capes and coats!

Socks and scarves!

Tutus and T-shirts!

Masks and more!

Everybody knows that superheroes work
all day to keep the world safe.

You can find superheroes:
In the store!

On the swings!

In the library!
On the stoop!

Everybody knows that superheroes fight
bad guys everywhere.

And everybody knows
that bad guy goo . . .

What a disaster!

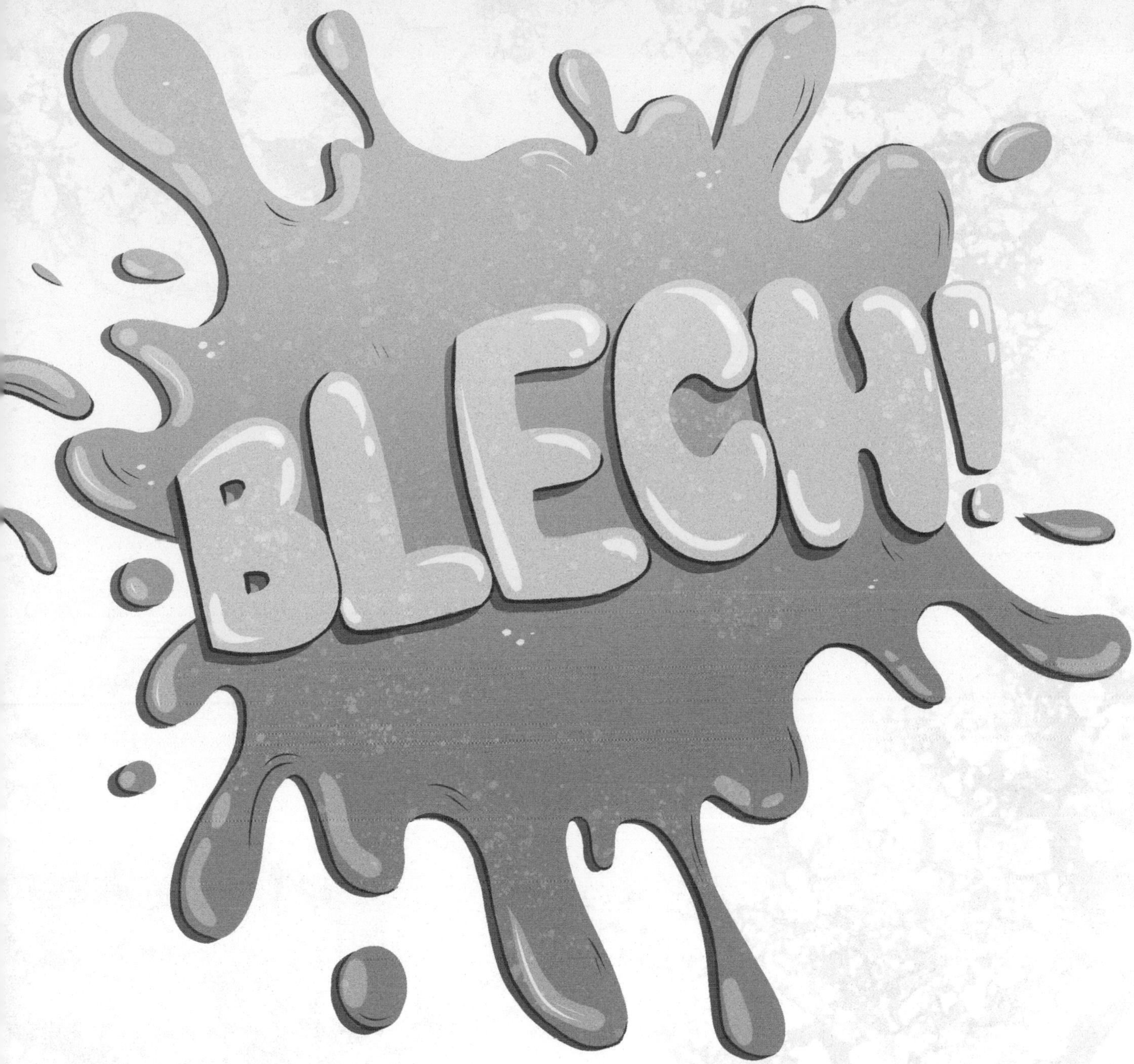
BLECH!

But the day isn't over
for superheroes like you.

Everybody knows that superheroes need to:

Recharge their bodies!

Wash off bad guy goo!

Relax their muscles!

Rest their minds!

And everybody knows
that superheroes:
Eat their dinner!

Take a bath!

Brush their teeth!

Read a book!

And everybody knows that superheroes: Need sleep!

In a bed!
Upside down!

In a spaceship!
Right-side up!

CITY NEWS

DAY SAVED AGAIN!

CITY HERO!

Tomorrow you'll save the day again.
And everybody knows . . .

. . . that you're the best superhero:

On the block!

In the neighborhood!

In the city!

In the world!